# UNKNOWN EVIL
# A STORY

# UNKNOWN EVIL
# A STORY

BY
RONALD R HIGGINS

Kravitz & Sons
INNOVATORS IN PUBLISHING, MARKETING AND ADVERTISING

**Kravitz and Sons LLC**
1301 Farmville Blvd, Suite 104
Greenville, NC 27834



Published by Kravitz and Sons LLC.

ISBN:        979-8-89639-007-7 (sc)
ISBN:        979-8-89639-006-0 (e)

Library of Congress Control Number: 2025904098

# Table of Contents

# DEDICATION

T his one is dedicated to My Niece Carol G and my friend Carol K for their help and support with this story.

# CHAPTER ONE

It was a cold winter night; the wind was whistling through the cracks of the old brownstone house. The house was built in the 1880s. New York winters were notoriously cold, but this house seemed to make everything feel icy-cold. Tom had gone to bed early because the electricity had gone out. There was a storm in the area, and there were no candles. Tom always kept candles in the house, but the last black-out took all the candles he had, and he had forgotten to buy more. Thank goodness blackouts only happened once in a while, usually at night and in winter when New York is at its coldest. The wind howled so hard the kitchen window blew out and wrenched Tom from an otherwise sound sleep. He walked down the stairs wishing he had a candle lighting the way. All of a sudden, the lights in the house flashed on and off, and on and off again. Tom knew in an instant that lightning had struck the electric box again. Tom tripped in the darkened hallway, going toward the kitchen and fell hard on the floor. As Tom got up, he felt something warm oozing down the side of his face; there was no mistaking the feeling of warm blood. While wiping it from the bottom of his face, he heard a terrifying sound from the kitchen.

He slowly walked toward the sound. As he passed the living room, he saw his father's shotgun hanging over the mantle of the fireplace. His father took it with him when he went hunting up-state New York; it was one of the few things he left him when he died. Tom went to the mantle, took the gun down, and then went to his desk to get the shells. As he loaded the rounds in the firearm, he heard that same blood-curdling sound, only this time it sounded closer. Tom hurried to load the gun. As he put the last shell in the barrel and pumped the first shell in the chamber, a big human-like hand reached over the desk. It grabbed the gun by the barrel and, in one twist, broke it in half. The room was dark except for the reflection of a streetlamp from outside. The creature then picked Tom up and threw him out the window, down onto the street.

When the police arrived, they found Tom dead, and his neck had been broken. They checked out the old brownstone and found nothing. The incident fell between the cracks of the news media until the following month when a similar crime happened on the Upper East Side. An older woman was found dead. It seemed she fell or was thrown out of the second-story window of her apartment, landing on Third Avenue her neck had been broken too. The  police had no clues on either incident.

The next two weeks went by uneventful, and then on the third week, they found the body of a police officer on west seventy-ninth. His head was twisted off his body and found about thirty yards away, near a trash can. Now the police were getting concerned. Somebody was not only going around killing innocent people, but now it was a Policeman. The police were afraid there would be a city-wide panic, especially if the media decided to have a field day.

Lt. Edward Stevens was assigned to the case; he had been with force for ten years. He was thirty-two years old and was born on Staten Island. Stevens graduated from N.Y.U. Then joined the police force afterward. Back then, the television was his blackboard, and the cops and robber programs were his books, Mike Hammer was his favorite detective. He stood about five foot eleven and weighed 180 pounds. Stevens loved milkshakes and had one whenever he could. He was one of those lucky people that never gained weight. Stevens has wanted to be a policeman since the killing of his father in the Red Hook section of Brooklyn. On her deathbed, his mother tried to talk him out of it. "Don't be like your father." She said, "Be anything but a Policeman." It was not to be.

Stevens wanted to be a Policeman. It is what he wanted most. Now here he was in the chief's office asking if Lt. Donald Rizzo could work with him on this one. They were roommates at the Academy. Stevens knew they would work well together. The Chief did not care, as long as he got results, fast. They soon became known as the C and R team, Collect and Research. The first couple of weeks were devoted to collecting data from the three previous murders and researching for clues. In the meantime, another crime had been committed; the neck broke just like the rest. There was one difference with this murder. A female Gorilla was found dead in her cage at the Central Park Zoo. The doors to the cage had been ripped off from the outside. The Creature that was committing these crimes did not distinguish between humans and animals. It was beginning to sound like a Stephen King novel. The Chief was getting pressure from his superiors, and he was passing the flack down to Stevens and Rizzo.

At the end of three weeks, the chief called them back in his office and asked them what they found out so far. Stevens started to speak:

"Well, chief, it's like this, Rizzo and I have followed up on every lead that we could, with the same results."

"What's that, Stevens?"

"Nothing chief, we've hit nothing but dead ends. The only thing we know for sure is that theirs been four brutal murders, and one was an Ape!"

"You mean to sit there and tell me you haven't found anything, motive or pattern?"

"Well, there is a pattern. For example, one, the murders were committed every Thirty days, and two all the victims died of broken necks."

The Chief was standing next to his desk, saying, "My superiors are on top of this one. They are watching to see what we do next."

Stevens says, "In case you didn't know it, chief, this Friday will be the end of another thirty days. That means if our theory is correct, our killer will strike again, in three days, only we don't know where or when."

The sound of the chief was ringing in Steven's ear as he walked out of his office. He and Rizzo decided to go back to square one and visit the house where the first murder took place. It was night, Tuesday night at about eight-thirty pm when they pulled up in front of the brownstone house in Brooklyn Heights; they found a light on in the second-story window.

"Say, Rizzo; I thought this place was closed up after the police had gone over it for clues."

"That's what I thought."

They both headed up the stairs to the front door; Stevens rang the bell. A few minutes had passed before they heard someone coming down to open the door. The front doors were like something out of the early 20th century; you know the kind of doors that has a rectangular glass-stained window on each entrance. They could see the reflection of the lighted candle as it floated down the stairs. The shadow of a woman accompanied the flashlight. The door opened, there in the doorway stood this vision of loveliness. She looked to be in her mid-thirties. She had long brown hair and stood about five foot four. She spoke, "Yes, may I help you?"

Stevens introduced Rizzo and himself, showing her his badge.

"May we come in and ask you a few questions?"

"Yes, of course, please come in." She showed them to the living room and then offered them some tea.

"No, thanks. This won't take long." Stevens says. "What would you like to know?" As she spoke, she went over and sat in a Queen Ann chair near the bookshelf, putting her hands in her lap.

"Well, first, I'd like to know who you are, I mean, we thought this place was locked up tight after the murder."

"I'm sorry, my name is Margie Spenser Tom was my older brother."

"Your last name is Spenser, and the murder victim's last name was Mead, I assume then you are married?"

"I'm a widow; my husband had been killed five years ago, in a subway accident."

"I am sorry," Stevens said.

"That's quite all right, what else would you like to know?"

"How long have you been living here, and who permitted you to occupy the place? The house is still a crime scene."

"When the police notified me of my brother's death, I took the plane down from Boston the next day."

"What are you doing here? I mean who permitted you to occupy the house, it's still under investigation?"

"I assumed it was okay to stay until all this business was finished."

"I guess it will be all right for now. Do you plan on selling the house?"

"I haven't decided yet; there are so many things about Tom's stuff, I'm trying to straighten out. Tom was such a collector of useless things. I don't know how he managed to fill up all the rooms with books and things in the three short years he's been living here, and most of the things are just junk and books on the occult."

When Ms. Spenser mentioned books on the occult, Stevens and Rizzo looked at each other with the same thought. The murders were not your regular run of the mill killings. That idea had been overlooked during the primary investigation.

"Ms. Spenser, do you mind if Rizzo and I go through some of that junk you mentioned?"

"Well...it's a little late tonight. Would you mind coming by in the morning?"

Lt. Stevens was thinking of what the chief had said about the killer striking in three days. Tomorrow would give them a two-day deadline.

"Sure, Ms. Spenser, that will be fine. We will see you first thing in the morning, around ten- thirty. Okay?"

She agreed.

When Rizzo and Stevens re-entered the street, they could feel the cold wind as it blew passed them from the east river. Stevens looked up and saw some dark, ominous-looking clouds pass over the light of the moon.

"Hey Stevens, you realize this Friday is Halloween?"

Stevens is looking at Rizzo with a smirk on his face, "You're just a mountain of information Rizzo. I know Friday is Halloween. I also know we have to catch the killer by Friday. I have an eerie feeling about those books Ms. Spenser told us about."

"Me too."

"We better get home and get some sleep. Something tells me we're going to have a busy day tomorrow."

# CHAPTER TWO

Wednesday, Oct. 29th morning.

The sun rises fast when you do not want it to. From Stevens's window, you could see the fiery red ball as it peeked between the city buildings marking the start of another day. Stevens could not help but think there is a killer out there someplace, and if he is not stopped by Friday, he is going to strike again. Stevens got up and called Rizzo and told him he would meet him at the diner on East Fourteenth Street for breakfast. Then he jumped into the shower.

When he arrived at the diner, it was nine o'clock in the morning. Rizzo was waiting outside. Stevens always felt sorry for Rizzo; his life started on the wrong foot. His father was Italian, and his mother was Jewish, what a combination. He was always hungry for Italian food, but still too cheap to pay for it. I do not think his mother knew how he dressed either. He always looked as if he slept in his clothes. He needed a keeper. Rizzo graduated from Hunter College then went to the Academy, where he and Stevens met. I think his problem was that he has never been outside of the city. Rizzo loved the city and everything it had to offer. He had no desire to go or visit any other place.

Rizzo's parents were originally from Philly. They moved here when Rizzo was ten; his father was a salesman. The Company transferred his father here to the primary office. Rizzo was glad because he was closer to the rest of the family.

Stevens parked the car and got out. He could see the meter maid writing tickets and putting them on the vehicles in front of him. She looked up long enough to wave, smile, and say good morning. Her name was Tracy; she had been with the city for three years. Stevens had a run-in with her on her first day. She ticketed his car while he was making an arrest; they have been friends ever since. Her ambition in life is to eventually become a detective, gold shield, and all that goes with it. She was taking some night courses to speed up the process. Rizzo, looking like his usual self-singled Stevens to hurry. They went inside and sat at a booth when Mable, the waitress, was coming over with some coffee.

"Morning guys, ready for another day of ridding the world of villains?"

Stevens looked up at Mable and said with a grin, "Mable, I see you got up on the right side of the bed this morning. Has your husband left you yet?"

"Hell, no, I kicked him out of the house last week. He took up too much of the bed." She was laughing as she walked away. Stevens and Rizzo looked at each other and laughed too. Gradually their smiles left. They were replaced by the realization that today was Wednesday. They had two days until the killer would strike again.

"Well, Stevens, what's first?"

"First, we eat. I do not like tracking killers on an empty stomach. Then we're going over to see Margie Spenser about some old books."

After breakfast, they headed over to Brooklyn Heights. Traffic at that time of the morning is pretty light. People are still heading toward Manhattan. When they arrived at Ms.

Spenser's house, the sun had already started to peek through the structure of the Brooklyn Bridge. There was a chill in the air that told you winter was just around the corner. As they stood in front of the door, waiting for Ms. Spenser to answer, Stevens had the strangest feeling that something was wrong. When Ms. Spenser finally opened the door, she had a frightened look on her face. Stevens asked, "Ms. Spenser, are you all right?"

"I'm not sure Lt. Won't you come into the house? I have something I want to show you." They followed her down the hall into the den. She went to what looked like a wall filled with books. She removed one particular book, and the wall moved aside, revealing an entrance to a tunnel or passageway. Ms. Spenser handed Stevens a flashlight and said: "You are welcome to investigate the passageway if you want, but I'm not going in there. I discovered it by accident last night. I was looking for something to read. I pulled this book from the shelf, and it triggered the wall, and it opened like this. I was too afraid to go inside. I put the book back, and it closed."

"That's all right, Ms. Spenser, my partner, and I will take it from here."

"C'mon Rizzo this is where we earn our pay." Stevens turned the flashlight on and headed down the dark corridor. When they made their way down the first part of the passage, they could smell the damp, pungent odor of sewer water. The walls were moist and cold. Stevens shined the light along the wall and on the ground; he spotted a sizeable water-rat scurrying down the narrow passageway and disappearing in the darkness.

"Hey, Stevens, that looked like something you dated last week."

"Hilarious Rizzo, I was with you, keep your eyes open. We don't know what's down here."

Just then, Stevens stopped and looked down. There in front of him was a stone, twisting, staircase leading farther down into the darkness. "Rizzo, it feels like it is getting warmer."

"Yeah, I know I was about to tell you the same thing, Stevens."

Just then, a scream was heard from the den, followed by, "Help, Help!"

"Quick Rizzo, that sounds like Ms. Spenser."

Stevens and Rizzo turned around and headed back toward the opening in the wall. When they arrived back at the entrance to the den, no one was there. They searched the rest of the house without finding Ms. Spenser. Stevens called the station house requesting a backup to help explore the tunnel. By evening they had discovered that the tunnel leads to an old, abandoned subway system that looked like it had not been used in fifty years. Whoever or whatever took Ms. Spenser was smart enough to know it would take forever to find her. It was getting late; the police stopped the search for the night; they would pick it up again in the morning. Stevens had a couple of the boy's downtown checking city hall for records and maps of the old subway system. In the meantime, Rizzo and Stevens went to check out the room where Ms. Spenser said her brother kept all his books on the occult. An hour had gone by when Stevens came across something strange.

"Hey Rizzo, what do you make of this?"

Stevens handed Rizzo a book with some bizarre writings in it. Rizzo took the book and started reading it. After a few minutes, he looked up at Stevens. "Shit, I can't make heads or tails of it, but it looks like some instructions or something. The writing is terrible. What is this book anyway?"

Stevens speaks, "It looks like some kind of notes that the brother was keeping. I'm getting a bizarre feeling about this whole case."

Rizzo chimed in, "I'll bet my cousin would know about this stuff. She's majoring in Parapsychology and Greek mythology at N.Y.U."

Stevens looked at his watch then at Rizzo. "What do Parapsychology and Greek mythology have to do with this case?"

"Well," Rizzo continued, "Ms. Spenser did say her brother had a lot of books on the occult, and this book is written funny, so I thought there might be a connection."

Stevens did not seem surprised that Rizzo made sense with his connecting the two; after all, he did graduate from Hunter

College and wondered why he had not thought of it first. Maybe he did but did not want to believe what he was thinking. "Is your cousin home now, maybe you can give her a call and ask if we could come over tonight?"

"I'll call and find out if she's home." Rizzo pulled out his cell phone and speed-dialed his cousin. She answered on the third ring. "Hello, Carol? Rizzo, I need a favor, yes, tonight. Can we come over right away? It is especially important. What do you mean, who are we? My partner and I, of course. Yeah, thanks." He hung up and looked at Stevens and gave him the thumbs-up sign. "Let's go, she'll see us now."

Stevens called in and told the Captain where they were headed. He did not give the Captain a chance to say no; he just hung up. They took off. On the way, Stevens started asking Rizzo some questions about his cousin Carol.

"So, tell me, Rizzo, how long has your cousin been going to N.Y.U.?"

"Carol Roselle? Well, it seems like forever, but she is in her next to last year. She's going for a doctorate in Parapsychology."

"What is she, a witch doctor?"

"No, Stevens, she's just into the paranormal and Greek Mythology, that's all."

"The Para. what?"

"Paranormal, you know, not within the range of normal experience."

Smiling, Stevens says, "I know if she has to deal with you, she has to deal outside the range of normal experiences." Stevens laughs sarcastically. "Okay, Stevens, you had your little laugh."

"C'mon Rizzo, you know I am just busting your hump. After about fifteen minutes, Stevens says we are almost there, right? It's' getting late, and her husband isn't going to mind having late visitors, is he?"

"Oh, she's not married I don't think she's even got a guy. She doesn't have time for relationships."

It was nine-thirty in the evening when they finally arrived at her apartment in Queens. She lived right off the L.I.E. near Citi-Park Stadium. It took forever to find a parking space in that part of town. They got lucky and found a spot; they parked and went inside. She lived on the third floor of a friendly apartment complex. Stevens and Rizzo took the elevator up to the third floor and knocked on the door. A few minutes passed, then the door opened and, in the doorway, stood this redheaded woman about five-five with a beautiful figure. She was wearing jeans and a button- down shirt and slippers. She smiled at Rizzo and spoke, "C'mon in, Shrimp."

She stepped aside and opened the door to let Rizzo and Stevens in. Stevens tapped Rizzo on the shoulder and said, "Shrimp?"

"Don't ask," Rizzo said.

Rizzo and Stevens followed Carol toward the living room; they could see the decor of the apartment. The kitchen walls were painted a bright yellow. The curtains over the sink looked like something out of Better Homes and Gardens. It gave the kitchen that homey look. You could tell a lot of time and money went into the living room. The living room floors were parquet. It looked as if you could eat off the flooring. There was a big oval throw rug in the middle of the room. There was just enough furniture in the room to give it class. The furniture was modern.

Stevens and Rizzo sat on the couch, while Carol sat across from them in a lounge chair. Carol was in her late twenties. She was an incredibly attractive woman.

"So, tell me, Shrimp, what's on your mind?"

"C'mon Carol, this is official business, call me Rizzo." "Okay, Rizzo, what's up?"

"This is my Partner, Lt. Stevens."

Stevens extended his hand and shook Carol's hand. They looked at each other and smiled.

"Hello, Ms. Roselle, nice to meet you. I hope we're not putting you out too much."

"No, of course not anything for shorty er... I mean, Rizzo. How can I help you?"

Stevens handed Carol the book, saying, "I thought maybe you could look at this book and tell us something about it. We could not make head or tails of it." Carol took the book and gave Stevens an interesting look. Then she opened it and started reading. After a few minutes, Carol stopped.

She looked up at Rizzo and then to Stevens. "Say, where did you get this anyway?"

Stevens spoke, "We think it may have something to do with the case we're working on."

"If it does, you guys may be in a lot of trouble." "What do you mean?"

"Well, Lt. Stevens, these writings look like incantations of some sort. I'd have to do some more studying before I could say for sure."

Stevens looked at Rizzo and back to Carol. "Please, Ms. Roselle, call me Stevens. How much time are we talking about because we do not have much to give? We have reason to believe the killer will strike again on Friday." "That only gives you two days," Carol says with surprise. "We know that that's why we're here now instead of tomorrow."

Carol looked at both of them and said, "Well, can you give me a few minutes to research this?"

"You got it," Stevens says.

"Why don't you guys go through that door to the kitchen and fix yourselves a drink there is some coffee on if you want it. I always keep a hot coffee pot for when I am up late studying. Give me about a half an hour to see what I can find out."

"C'mon Stevens let's see what she has in the fridge."

"No, thanks. You go on; I'll stay here." Looking at Carol, he says, "That is if your cousin doesn't mind."

"No, of course not please Stevens call me Carol."

Rizzo turned and headed for the kitchen. Carol looked up at Rizzo and said, "Hey Rizz, there's a banana cream pie in there, if you want it." She smiled at Stevens as she said that. Stevens looked at Carol and shook his head and smiled. "I don't think you should encourage him. When was the last time you saw your cousin turn down food?"

"Never, that's why I told him. I have been trying to get rid of it so that I would not eat it myself. A woman has to watch her figure these days."

Stevens took a long look at Carol from top to bottom, ending up looking into her eyes. "From where I'm sitting, your figure doesn't look like it needs watching."

Carol smiled at him, embarrassingly. "Ah, well, yes, that's another story."

Stevens says, "I would like to hear about it sometime." Carol replied, "Aren't you just a little bit forward?" Stevens smiled now he was feeling a little uncomfortable about what he had just said, and continued, "Well, I'll leave you alone so you can study that information for us."

Stevens got up and went into the kitchen. When he entered the kitchen, he sees Rizzo bent over the refrigerator. "Hey Rizzo, give your cousin a break, will you? She's doing us a favor, and you're cleaning out her fridge."

Rizzo stood up and turned around. He has mustard on the side of his mouth. "Hey, I'm just looking for a beer."

Forty-five minutes had gone by, and Stevens was getting impatient. Rizzo had stuffed himself and was sitting at the kitchen table, ready to fall asleep. Just then, a voice came from the other room.

"Hey guys, come on back, I think I found something you might be interested in."

Stevens and Rizzo came in from the kitchen and sat on the couch.

Carol starts, "This is going to be a little hard for you to swallow but try anyway.

Rizz, do you know anything about Greek Mythology or the occult?"

"No, Carol, I don't. Rizzo turns to Stevens; how about you, Stevens?"

"If you mean do, I believe in witches and goblins, no, I don't."

Carol replies, "Stevens, there are a lot of unexplained things in this world. Some things are impossible to explain, but people believe in them anyway, because of tradition." Stevens looked at Carol and replies, "Like what?"

Carol answers with, "Well, for example, Santa Claus, or the Easter Bunny. People know there are no such characters. Some people believe in them because it suits their purpose at the time. At Christmas, people like to believe there's a Santa Claus because it makes them feel good and puts them in the spirit of giving."

"What's your point?"

"Do you believe in God, Mr. Stevens?" "Well...er... yes, of course, I do." "Why?"

"Why well because...er... you're supposed to. I mean, I was raised that way."

"What proof do you have that there is a god?" "No proof, it is just faith."

"Exactly, what I'm about to tell you was based on faith a long time ago."

"Is this going to take long?" Rizzo said.

"Not very, but you must listen to it with an open mind. If you are going to understand what I think is happening, happened."

"Go on."

"Have you ever heard of a Minotaur?"

Stevens speaks, "A Minotaur, yes, wasn't he some kind of god that the Greeks believed in?"

"Not exactly, the Greeks believed stories about an island called Crete and the king of that Island was called Minos. Stories of

Minos and the ceremonies and practices of Cretan Bull Worship were spread widely about the Mediterranean at that time. There is, for example, the Greek legend of Europa and the bull. The maiden Europa was seduced and taken across the sea. To the island of Crete by the god Zeus in the form of a bull. There she gave birth to Minos, who later became the Bull-god-King of the Island."

Stevens was all caught up in Carol's little story. Rizzo did not like any of it.

"Carol, we don't have time for all of this. Can't you tell us what the writings mean?"

"Shut-up, Rizzo said Stevens; I want to hear it." "Thank you, Mr. Stevens."

"Go on, Carol, and call me Stevens."

Carol continued, "The Minotaur was the result of the union between the wife of Minos, and a bull which she had become infatuated. By concealing herself within a wooden cow, constructed for her by the master craftsman Daedalus, she had seduced the bull. Minos imprisoned the man-bull creature that she bore in a Labyrinth at Cnossos, and it was here that the young Athenians met their end."

"What has this got to do with this case?"

"Well, let's take these writings you gave me in this book." "What about them?"

"They are formulas or incantation if you will; to call forth the Minotaur into the present."

Now Rizzo was getting excited. He did not believe what he was hearing. "What!!"

"Let me get this straight, Carol." Stevens continued, "You're saying these writings somehow caused a Minotaur to be transported from the past to the present?"

"No, the formulas or incantations in this book call the Minotaur to the present. I'm not saying they did."

"Carol, you're giving me a frightening twist to my problem. You know that, don't you?"

"It's just one of many possible solutions to your dilemma. I'm just telling you what the writings in this book say."

"I know Carol, and I appreciate the suggestion, but..."

Just then, Rizzo chimed in, "Well Stevens, I think this whole thing is bull shit if you will pardon my French, and I don't believe a word of it."

Carol speaks, "Thanks, Rizz, you always were articulate when it came to express yourself."

"Ah, come on, Carol, you don't expect us to swallow that shit."

"Rizzo, you came here asking me for my help. I'm sorry I didn't tell you what you wanted to hear."

Through this whole confrontation between Rizzo and Carol, Stevens sat there thinking about what Carol had told them. "Hold on, everybody. Now, wait a minute Rizzo. When murders of this nature occur, people who are concerned with solving them have to have a place to start. Through a multitude of theories combined with concrete evidence, they end up with the most valid solution. When all else is proven, untrue whatever is left is probable. In part, that is what we are trying to do here. Now let us keep our wits about us."

"All right, Stevens, but I still think it is bull shit." Rizzo was mad.

Stevens turned to Carol, smiled, and said, "Thank you for your time. I know you're a remarkably busy person, and it was nice of you to see us."

"Stevens, if you don't mind, I would like to assist you in this case. That is if it's all right with you."

Stevens looked at her for a minute and smiled.

"Well, we could use your expertise in this matter, but I must warn you. The police cannot pay you for your services, and we can't be responsible for your safety."

"That's quite all right; the experience I can pick-up will be invaluable to me toward my doctorate."

"Well, I appreciate your offer. Why don't I give you a call tomorrow after I've looked into this further?"

"Fine, that sounds great."

Carol writes down her phone number and gives it to Stevens. Rizzo followed Stevens to the door and turned back toward Carol.

Rizzo turned at the door and said, "Thanks, Carol, I still think you're a little strange, but I still love you, and thanks for your help."

"Rizz, I love you too."

On the way down in the elevator, Rizzo could not get what Carol had said out of his mind.

"Stevens, you don't believe that bull shit Carol was feeding us, do you?"

"Listen, Rizzo; I'm only going to say this once. A good investigator keeps an open mind about all theories until they are proven the truth or proven totally out of the question. So far, nothing is ruled out."

"Okay, partner, I don't believe that, but I'm with you all the way. What's next?"

"I know this is going to sound crazy but let us keep this theory to ourselves for the time being. I do not want to be the butt of a lot of jokes at the station house. Not yet, anyway."

"That's the first bit of sense you've made so far."

# CHAPTER THREE

Thursday - 9 a.m.

Stevens had just gotten out of the shower and was getting dressed when the phone rang, he picked up the phone and said hello. He heard a female voice answer, and he recognized Carol's voice. "Hi, Carol, what's going on? Wait a minute. How did you get my number?"

"I called the station and told them I was working with you on this case, and they were glad to give it to me. I hope you don't mind; I was just so excited about working with you on this case I couldn't wait."

"Carol, I wished you would have waited until I spoke to the Captain about this"

"I'm sorry I just thought this was important and I wanted to ask you if I could go to the house when you go again."

Stevens thinks for a moment and then says, "I guess there wouldn't be any harm in that. I'll pick you up outside your place in an hour."

"Okay, I'll be ready. Bye."

Stevens hangs up and calls Rizzo to tell him to meet him over at the house in Brooklyn Heights. Rizzo says, "O.k. But first I have to go to the station house and fill out some paperwork. I will meet you at the house afterward."

When Stevens pulled up in front of Carol's apartment in Queens, she was waiting for him out front. She was standing there wearing jeans and a tank top and low heels.

Carol was carrying a jacket. This woman was one of the few women he had seen in recent years that could wear jeans well. She climbed in, and they headed for Brooklyn Heights. Stevens's curiosity got the best of him. He wanted to know more about Carol, so he asked. "So, tell, me Carol, have you ever been married?"

Carol looked at him, smiled, and said, "Boy, you don't waste any time you ask the big questions first. No, how long have you lived in the city or where are you from, etc."

Stevens is a little embarrassed by the way his question came out, tried to regroup. "I'm sorry I didn't mean it the way it sounded; I was trying to start a conversation. I need to get out more often."

Carol laughed, "On no, that's okay. I married a young eighteen. It did not last long, though; I divorced him at nineteen. It turns out he liked to use me as a punching bag from time to time whenever he had come home drunk, which was often. The good news is that we never had any kids."

"Did you want kids?"

Carol looked at Stevens and smiled and continued, "Still do as soon as I found the right man. Until then, I am concentrating on getting my doctorate. What about you?" "Oh, I was married once, but it didn't work out. No kids." "She beat you, huh?" Carol says with a smile.

Stevens looks back at her and smiles and then says, "No, just differences of opinions. She wanted me to change jobs, and I wanted to be a cop. So, we went our separate ways."

"Do you regret your decision?" Carol says. "No, not at all. What about you?"

"Nope, I went out and took some Karate lessons and got on with my life."

They arrived at Ms. Spenser's house at ten a.m. On the way over, Stevens had filled

Carol in on the case. There was a young Patrolman at the front door. As Stevens and Carol approached, he picked up his list of people permitted into the crime scene and asked for some I.D. Stevens took out his badge and flashed it at the patrolman. At the same time, he asked him his name.

The patrolman looked at him and said, "Patrolman Hogan, sir."

Stevens pointing to Carol, said, "Well, Hogan, this young lady here is with me. She will be working on the case with me and Lt. Rizzo. When Lt. Rizzo arrives, tell him I'm inside with Ms. Roselle Waiting."

"Yes, sir." Then looking at Carol, he says, "Nice meeting you." Looking back at Stevens, he says, "I'll Notify Lt. Rizzo when he arrives, sir."

As they entered the house, Stevens led Carol down the hallway toward the kitchen. Stevens stopped when they reached the entrance to the living room and showed

Carol where Tom Mead was thrown through the window on to the street. From there, they went on to the den where Ms. Spenser disappeared. When they entered the room, another guard approached them.

"Good morning, Lt."

Stevens knew the officer from past cases. "Morning, Jack. How's it going?"

"Fine, Lt. nice and quiet."

"Jack, this is Carol Roselle, she is assisting me in this case. Carol, this is Patrolman Saunders."

"Hello, Jack Saunders."   "Hello, Ms. Roselle."

Carol followed Stevens over to the open wall to the tunnel. Just then, Rizzo entered the hallway with some papers in his hand. He was pretty excited.

"Say, Stevens..." Just then, Rizzo spotted his cousin, waves at her, then continued,

"Carol, I didn't know you were going to be here."

Stevens speaks, "Well, she wanted to see the house, so I picked her up this morning. What did you find out?"

Rizzo, still excited, said, "Wait until you see what I've got here." Rizzo goes to the desk and spreads the papers out and starts to explain. "These just happen to be Photostat copies of the old subway system under the city."

"Old? I thought there was only one subway system in New York."

"That's just it, very few people knew about this other system. It started around the turn of the century. About 1901, after about six months of building, they decided to close up that route and start over from square one." "How did you find that out?"

"My uncle used to work for the city planning commission." He turns to Carol and says, "Carol, you remember Uncle Joe."

"Oh yeah, Uncle Joe, he and Aunt Martha separated when we were small," Carol said.

"That's the one, anyway, when I told him about this tunnel, he made a call to a friend at city hall and got these Photostats for me."

The Photostats showed everything except the entrance to the subway from the tunnel. After looking at the plans for about five minutes, Stevens walked away toward the books on the far wall. Rizzo looked up and watched Stevens for a minute. "Stevens, what's the matter?"

"Well, Rizzo, we still don't know how many tunnels there are before we get to the old subway system. Did the search squad find any maps when they searched this place?" "They searched for this place from top to bottom and found nothing."

Carol looks at Stevens and says, "Tell me, Stevens, did Tom Mead play golf?"

Stevens and Rizzo looked at each other with strange looks on their faces. Then Stevens says, "What does that have to do with anything?"

"Well, I have a brother who plays golf. When we were kids, and he wanted to hide anything, he would put it inside his golf bag. He still does today."

"Well, I don't know if he owned one or not, but we can check the inventory list the investigating team made up when they went through this place. Rizzo, why don't you check with the officer on duty and see if he has the list."

"Right, Stevens."

Rizzo leaves the room to check with the officer; Stevens looks over at Carol. She is bending over the table, staring at the map. Stevens notices her body and how attractive she is. At that moment, Carol looks up at Stevens and sees him peering at her. His face went flushed, knowing he had just gotten caught in an awkward situation.

Carol smiles at him and says, "Like what you see?" "No ah yeah not bad, not bad at all, how about dinner tonight?"

"I don't know, are you safe?"

"If I'm not, you can call a cop."

"Oh, that's good, a police detective with a sense of humor."

Then Rizzo comes back with the inventory list and gives it to Stevens. Stevens reads it. "Well, well, well. It seems the newest addition to our investigative team hit upon something. Mr. Mead does have a golf bag in the upstairs closet, let us go." Stevens and Carol hurried out the door and up the stairs, followed close behind by

Rizzo. Stevens opened the closet door, and there in the back of the closet was a set of golf clubs right down to the bag.

"Bingo," Stevens said. As he took the clubs out of the closet and looked down inside the golf bag, he saw something. He took the clubs out and reached his hand down inside again and pulled out a large roll of paper. Stevens looked at Carol with a big grin and said, "I could kiss you."

Carol looks back at him shyly, her face slightly red. Rizzo looking at both of them says, "C'mon guys let's be serious, party later."

Stevens says. "Rizzo, you're right. Let us go down to the den and see if we can make something out of this."

When they get to the den, Stevens spreads the map out on the desk. Looking at the legend, Stevens notices the year the map was printed. "Rizzo, look at the date on this map." Rizzo looks at the date.

"Nineteen-five holy shit, I wonder where he got this map."

"I'd like to find out when that tunnel was connected to the old subway route," Stevens says.

The guard at the door in front calls Stevens. "Lt. Stevens, there is a man at the front door that wants to see Tom Mead."

Stevens looked at Carol and Rizzo with a surprised look on his face. "Okay, Jack, I'll be right out." Turning to Rizzo, he says, "You and Carol check this map out and see how many of these tunnels lead to the subway. I'll be right back."

Stevens walked out of the den and headed for the front door with some concern. When he reached the door and opened it, he saw a tall man of about six-foot standing and talking to the officer. The man was trying to find out what has going on and why the police were here.

"Excuse me, sir. I am Lt. Stevens I am the investigating officer in charge. Can I help you?"

"Yes, my name is Bob Mead. Tom Mead is my brother, and he owns this house. What are you doing here? What's going on anyway?"

"Mr. Mead, do you live in New York?"

"Yes, I do, but I've been out of the country for the last couple of months on business."

"I see, and exactly what kind of business are you in?"

"I buy and sell Real Estate. Now look, I have answered your questions; will you please answer mine? What's going on?"

"Mr. Mead, I'm afraid I have bad news for you. Your brother has been murdered, and your sister has disappeared." The pale look and blank stare on Mr. Mead's face told Stevens he was not taking it very well.

"Mr. Mead, won't you come in, and I'll explain as best I can."

Stevens shows him into the Kitchen and begins to explain. "Mr. Mead, your brother was the first in a series of bizarre murders. Your brother was discovered on Aug. 8th by a passerby, out in front of this house. He was dead of a broken neck. It appeared as if he had been thrown from his window. We are looking into it now. About two days ago, your sister disappeared from this house. We're looking into that too."

"My brother is dead, and my sister is missing, and all you can say is you're looking into it?" Mr. Mead's expressions changed from sadness and concern to anger in two seconds flat. "I want your badge number and the name of your superior. I want something done immediately."

Mr. Mead sits back down and starts to cry. Just then, Carol and Rizzo enter the room and ask what is going on. "Everything is under control. Carol, Rizzo, I want you to meet Mr. Bob Mead. His brother is Tom Mead, and his sister is Ms. Spencer."

Bob Mead, aware now that there were two other people in the room, pulls himself together. He stands to greet them and says, "How do you do, I'm sorry for my behavior. It's just that; it's quite a shock for me to find out that my brother has been murdered, and my sister has disappeared."

Carol speaks, "We understand Mr. Mead, an apology isn't necessary. Lt's Stevens and Rizzo are doing everything possible to find out who the murderer is, and they are trying to find your sister. It is just that it is going to take time. Please be patient."

"Thank you, Miss... er er?"

Stevens speaks, "I'm sorry. Let me introduce you to Carol Roselle. She is assisting me in the case, and this is my partner. Lt. David Rizzo."

Bob Mead stands and shakes hands with Rizzo and Carol. "It's nice to meet you both. I want to thank all of you for what you are doing."

"No problem, Mr. Mead. Why do not you leave your name and address and the phone number where you can be reached, with the officer at the door, and we'll contact you as soon as we have something."

"Yes, of course."

Mr. Mead leaves the room. Stevens, Rizzo, and Carol all look at each other for a minute.

Carol speaks, "Stevens, do you think we will find the killer?"

Stevens, trying to sound positive, "Well, we're not going to do it standing around like this. But to answer your question, yes, I think we will." Turning to Rizzo, he says, "What did you find out about the tunnels?"

"Well, according to the map, Stevens, three of the passageways lead to three different parts of the old subway system. A fourth leads to an upstairs room."

"Good, we'll start with the room upstairs. Rizzo and I will take the tunnel route to the room. Carol, you see if you can find the room by going up the stairs. Check all the rooms. We'll all meet in one of them, I hope."

Carol heads up the stairs as Stevens and Rizzo head for the den and the passageway that will lead them to the room upstairs. When Rizzo and Stevens enter the den, they pick up the map at the desk, and Rizzo shows Stevens the way to the room on the map.

"Well Rizzo, that doesn't look difficult to follow, what do you say we take a shot at it?"

Stevens folds the map up and slips it in his inside jacket pocket, and they proceed toward the open wall.

When they went into the tunnel the first time, the day Ms. Spenser disappeared, they had gone left. According to the map, the passageway to the right should take them to the room upstairs. They shined their flashlights in that direction and headed up the corridor. Stevens had an uneasy feeling about this place as he and Rizzo advanced further and further into the tunnel. After a few minutes of traveling a slight incline, it leveled off. At that point, Stevens and Rizzo approached a doorway on the left, which opened to a small room with no windows. When Stevens and Rizzo entered the room, they could see on the left wall, chains with cuffs attached to them. The shackles were embedded in the wall, just like you would see in one of those old horror movies. They saw a small table and chair also in the room, on the table was a small oil lamp. The lamp was out, but the base still had oil in it, and the wick looked as though it had been used recently. Stevens and Rizzo left the room and headed up the passageway. Stevens turns to Rizzo and says, "You know Rizzo, the more I find out about this case, the less I know."

"Yeah, Stevens, I get the same feeling, this Tom Mead character was a strange one. I mean, he was a History teacher during the day at Hunter College, but on his own time, he was into some strange shit, you know the occult and black magic. It doesn't seem like a healthy way of life." After about another fifteen minutes of traveling the winding tunnel, they came to a dead end. On the wall facing Stevens was an odd-looking piece of chain hanging on the wall. "Well, Rizzo, what do you think, should I do the obvious, and pull the chain?"

"Stevens, I think that would be the usual response. I hope we don't get flushed!"

Stevens puts a slight smile on his face and pulls the chain down. At first, nothing happens, and Stevens pulls down on the chain again. This time there was a strange noise, and the wall began to move aside, revealing a room on the other side. Carol was standing in the center of the room.

"I didn't think you guys were going to make it," Carol says. "We weren't too sure ourselves when we started. You know, Carol, this is a bizarre house."

"You're telling me! While you guys were following the yellow brick road to Oz. I came across a book about the history of this house. For starters, did you know this house dates back to the early settlements? When George Washington was in office, and he lived down in the Wall Street area? Then, this house was owned by a Mister Malone, and you'll never guess what he did for a living." Stevens looks at Rizzo and back to Carol and says, "Don't tell me, he was a schoolmaster."

"How did you know?"

"I guess it was a lucky guess."

"Say, Stevens, tell Carol what a strange tunnel we just went through."

"You better get used to that tunnel, Rizzo. We're going back in after lunch."

"Ah Stevens, ya gotta be kidding."

"No, I'm not. Do not forget we have to find that killer before he finds his next victim. That is if he has not already. Remember, Ms. Spenser is still missing."

Carol speaks, "Do you think she's in the tunnel?"

"Well, Carol, the more I explore the tunnel, the more I suspect that there's something strange going on in that old subway system. The faster we get down there and check the place out, the better I will feel. What else can you tell me about Mr. Malone?"

"According to the book, Mr. Malone came here from Virginia with the money his folks left him when they died. He got a job as a Schoolmaster and used part of his inheritance to build this house. It's all here in his handwriting."

Carol hands Stevens a hard-covered book. All the pages have turned brown through the normal aging cycle. Stevens starts to read it and then looks at Rizzo and back to Carol. "Holy shit, you weren't kidding, this book looks like it's been around for some time."

He hands Carol back the book, "Tell me more."

"Strange as it may seem, Mr. Malone was also into black magic and the occult. He practiced witchcraft at night in this house. He was afraid of being found out, so as a precaution, he built that tunnel as an escape route. At the time, it led to the outskirts of the city."

"How did he finally die?" Rizzo asks.

"Well, Rizzo, oddly enough, he was found one morning in an alley not far from here. His head was missing. They never did find out who did it, and they never did find his head. The house was taken over by the city. According to Mr. Clay, who continued writing in the book when he purchased the house and found the book, shortly after the turn of the century, around nineteen-five a Mr. Clay bought the house from the city. He was excited about the city making plans to build a subway system, so he made sure his tunnel had access to it so he would have an exit from the house if the time came and he had to use it. When the city abandoned the project for a better one, Mr. Clay had a tunnel leading to an ex-future subway system, So much for Mr. Clay. Oh, there is one more thing."

"What is that, Carol?"

"Stevens, everyone that owned this house, has died or disappeared mysteriously. After Mr. Clay disappeared, the city never found him. They took over the house, and it was in their possession for about fifty years or so, at which time the city auctioned it off. That's when Mr. Mead finally bought the house in 1998."

"Doesn't sound at all like the kind of house I would want to live in," Rizzo says, with a grin on his face.

Stevens just looked at him with a mock smile.

"What do you say we break for lunch, guys? Rizzo, I will meet you back here at two. Carol and I are going to lunch." Carol looking at Stevens with a curious smile, "We are, since when?"

"Since now." Then he smiled and continued, "Well because, I just asked you, that's why."

"I didn't hear you ask me!"

"Well then, let me take you to lunch anyway."

Carol looked at Stevens and took a swing at him playfully and hit him on the arm. "Okay, Stevens, where are you taking me?"

Rizzo looks at both of them like they are crazy, shakes his head, and says, "I'll see you guys at two."

He turns and leaves, leaving Stevens and Carol staring at each other.

"Well, big spender, where are we going?" "I know just the place."

Stevens takes Carol by the arm and leads her out the door. On the way, Stevens tells the guard to hold down the fort until they get back. It had just started raining.

# CHAPTER FOUR

Thursday – Noon.

Carol and Stevens are sitting at a table by the window of the restaurant. It has the same one Stevens had been coming to for years, but Carol had never been there. It had been raining. You could see people putting newspapers over their heads to keep the rain out. Of course, some listened this morning, when the weatherman said, to bring your umbrella. It was only noon, but the sky was dark. The cars were driving down the streets, turning on their headlights and wipers. The lights were reflecting off the wet boulevards giving an eerie look to the streets.

"So, Stevens, tell me how long were you married?"

Stevens was watching the rain when Carol asked the question. This time Carol took Stevens by surprise, and he was taken aback by the question. Carol could see the unsettled look on his face. "I'm sorry we don't have to talk about it if you don't want to. I was trying to break the ice a little, that is all. I mean, we had talked about it in the car this morning. I didn't think you minded."

"No, that's all right. I do not mind talking about it. It was a long time ago; Gloria was her name. Shortly after I graduated from the Police Academy, we got married. Her folks were from New Rochelle; her father was a big doctor in charge of a hospital in New Rochelle. They had a lot of money. They did not want their daughter marrying a Policeman. She was supposed to marry into a rich family, to keep the tradition going, but we were young and in love."

Carol was starting to feel guilty about asking the question, but she wanted to know more. She liked Stevens and knew she had to find out more.

Stevens continued, "We thought getting married was the solution to everything. Talk about being naive. Anyway, things were great for the first year. We got a nice apartment on the Upper East Side; we were both working. I was working a beat in Brooklyn, up by the Verrazano Bridge. It was not a bad section, not like Red hook. Gloria was working with a marketing firm in mid-town Manhattan. Every month of the first year I was married, I sent her roses. The first month I sent one rose with a note that read; 'This is number one, smell it and have some fun.' The second month I sent two roses with a note that read; 'This is number two, boy I sure love you.' By the time I got to the end of the first year, I could not think of a rhythm that went with twelve, so I just sent her a dozen roses with a short note."

"How thoughtful, that was sweet," Carol said.

Stevens was beginning to feel a little embarrassed. He continued, "It was shortly after that first year that things started getting tough. It was about that time; they transferred six of us down to the Red Hook section of Brooklyn. I had to work a lot of extra shifts. The money was good, but I did not get to be with Gloria very much. When I did see her, I was so tired all I wanted to do was sleep. I guess she got lonely. Anyway, she found someone else."

Carol could see how much it still bothered Stevens to talk about it. As she spoke, she reached across with her hand and squeezed his hand. "I'm sorry, Stevens, really I am."

Stevens did not say anything; he just stared at Carol's hand, touching his and looked back at her eyes. They looked at each other for a moment, and suddenly they both realized this was not going to be just a working relationship. The waiter came and broke the mood, then left after taking their order. Wanting to change the subject, Carol asked, "Have you and Rizzo been partners long?"

"We met at the academy and have been together since. We have seen a lot of cases come and go, but this one is one of the strangest. Have you got any more theories?"

"I told you my theory the other night, I believe it even more now, after what I found out at home today."

"The book you mean."

"Yes, the book. The way the book had been written told me the man had a rather good education. A man with that kind of background wouldn't make up something like that."

"You don't think so?"

"No! Of course not, what reason would he have to lie?" Stevens jumps in with, "How about he's plain nuts to start with who says he has to have a reason? Half the people in this city are crazy."

"You don't believe what you're saying."

"Well, I can't speak for when that book was written. I'm only speaking for now."

Carol replies, "Knowing what you know about this case so far, can you honestly say you don't believe what's written in that book?"

"At this point, I don't know what to believe. All I know is someone or something is going around killing people, and I need to find out who it is and stop them before they kill again." Just then, the waiter came over with their order, and all talking stopped while they ate lunch and exchanged glances at each other.

Back at Mr. Mead's house, Rizzo just finished reading the diary. He notices the back cover has a slight rip, and there is a small fold of paper showing. He pulls it out. The piece of paper is newer than the pages of the book. He unfolds it and discovers that it is a map of the tunnel.

Looking at it further, he finds one passage that leads under the old subway system. He and Stevens had not seen that passageway when they went through the tunnel earlier in the day. He calls the restaurant and tells Stevens what he has uncovered. Stevens says he and Carol are on their way back. Rizzo hangs up the phone and goes back to the library to wait for Stevens. Rizzo, now standing by the desk, is looking over the two maps, the one from the city planning commission and the one he just found. Rizzo has his back to the bookshelf, so he does not see the wall open. Nor can Rizzo see the giant figure of a man-like creature that enters through the exposed wall and comes up behind him. With one swift move of his arm, he knocks Rizzo unconscious. Picking up the map of the tunnel that Rizzo discovered, he turns and goes back into the passageway and disappears.

Five minutes had passed by the time patrolman York made his periodic check inside the house and found Rizzo unconscious on the floor. Patrolman York helped Rizzo to the couch and went into the kitchen to get him some water. He came back, handed Rizzo the glass of water, and asked him what happened. Rizzo drank the water and said, "I don't know, one minute I was reading this map (as he points to where the map was, he realizes it's not there) where the hell did the map go? The map, the map it was right there on the table."

Patrolman York looks on the table and sees the map from the city planners. "There it is. Right there on the table."

Rizzo looks and says, "Not that one, the other one." Rizzo starts looking around the room.

"I don't know which one you are referring to. I only see one map. (Patrolman York points to the map on the table) Rizzo is furious "I'm not going crazy the map I'm talking about was on that table a minute ago along with the other map."

Stevens and Carol enter the room. "What's wrong Rizzo, your call sounded urgent?"

Rizzo runs over to Stevens and Carol. "I'm glad you guys are back."

"What's all this nonsense about another map?"

"It's gone."

"What's gone, Rizzo?"

"The other map that was on the table over there." Stevens looks and speaks, "The other map, what other map?"

"The other map I found here in the back binding of this book."

Rizzo takes the diary out of the draw and shows Stevens and Carol where the binding was torn. Stevens takes the book from Rizzo and examines it.

"So, where's the map?"

"That's what I'm trying to tell you. The map was stolen right out from under my nose."

"What are you talking about?"

Rizzo is getting upset now, and it shows. "Listen, you guys went to lunch, while you were gone, I started reading the diary. When I noticed the back-binding cover of the diary was torn. I checked it out, and that's when I found a map hidden inside the back cover."

"So, where is it?"

"Patience, and I'll tell you, Stevens." Rizzo continues, "While I was comparing the two maps on the table over there." Rizzo points in the direction of the table on the other side of the room. "Something or somebody came up from behind and slugged me."

Stevens turned and asked patrolmen York, "Did you see anybody enter or exit the front door in the last hour?"

"No, Sir. Nobody got by me. When I made my rounds, I found Lt. Rizzo lying there on the floor." He was unconscious. I went to the kitchen and got him a glass of water and help him to the couch.

Rizzo continued, "When I came to the map was gone." Suddenly everybody in the room looked toward the bookshelf wall. Rizzo speaks, "You don't suppose it was that creature that Carol was talking about, from that Island?"

Rizzo looked at Carol. Carol looked at Stevens, and Stevens looked back to Rizzo. Stevens and Carol headed toward the wall where the books were. Stevens moved the book that is the lever that used to control the wall, and the wall slowly started to open. As the wall opened, Stevens told Rizzo to stay and call for backup. Then he motioned for the patrolman to follow him. As he stepped into the passageway with the policeman, Carol followed. "Oh no, Carol, you're staying here. We don't know what to expect."

Carol replied, "All the more reason for me to go, you're going to need someone to translate anything you find down there."

Reluctantly Stevens agreed and said, "Okay, but stay right behind me. I don't want to have to worry about where you are."

Carol nodded in agreement; they started walking down the corridor, shining the flashlights in front of them. Stevens took the map he had out of his back pocket and looked at it quickly for reference and put it back in his pocket. While they made their way through the tunnels and passageways, Stevens wondered what was waiting for them. Suddenly one of the halls opened up to a full tunnel with half laid tracks on the ground. As they cross the tracks to the other side of the tunnel after a few minutes, they saw the light in the distance. It was coming toward them. They stood frozen in their tracks. Stevens was afraid the patrolman might fire before they could find out who or what it was. "Hold your fire until we're sure of who or what it is."

Just then, they heard a familiar voice.

"Stevens, is that you? Rizzo, what the hell are you doing down here? I thought I told you to wait for the backup."

"No, what you said was call for backup, and I did, they are on their way."

"How did you get here from that direction? What I mean is, how did you find us coming from that way?"

"Well, remember that map I told you about, well I remembered seeing another passageway leading to this same place. So, I followed it to see if I was right, and here I am." "Yeah, well, what else do you remember about that map?"

"Well, Stevens..." Rizzo looked around the tunnel and pointed to one of the doorways that lead into another passageway.

"This looks like the right one. Come on." They all follow Rizzo through the door and down the passage to another doorway. They could hear trains in the distance coming from the tunnels above.

"Rizzo, what are you looking for?"

"I'll tell you when I see it." Just then, they heard another familiar voice in the distance, yelling Stevens's name.

"Say, Rizzo, that sounds like the Captain's voice. The backup team must be here. Let us get back to the library."

Stevens turned, and they all headed back the way they came, Rizzo told them to wait; he knew a faster way, so Rizzo and Carol begin to follow him, and before you knew it, they were going through the entrance that leads them back into the library where the Captain was waiting for them. When they entered the room, the Captain was standing there with four uniformed Policemen.

"Well, Stevens, what's this all about?"

"Captain...ah. We may have a lead to all those bizarre murders."

"Oh... Stevens, you mean you guys weren't playing tag in an old tunnel."

The Captain was upset because he thought Stevens had been spending a lot of time on the case and not coming up with too many clues.

"No listen to Captain, Carol here is going for her doctorate at N.Y.U. in parapsychology, and she has been helping us with our investigation."

The Captain looked at Stevens and said, "May I remind you she is a civilian? Besides, how is she helping with the investigation?"

Stevens and Rizzo looked at each other, knowing full well the Captain was not going to buy the story but knowing that they had to tell him something to stall for more time to get some concrete evidence. "Well, we believe we're on the trail of a murderer that you would not believe if the truth were known to you at this time. All we ask is some time to sort out all the clues and leads."

The Captain looked at Rizzo, Stevens, and then to Carol. "Okay, Stevens, you take a couple of days off to collect your thoughts. Then you have seventy-two hours to come up with some hard evidence in this case, or I'm going to have to turn it over to the Chief, and you know how he's going to take it, now the two of you get on out of here and take this civilian with you."

Stevens, Rizzo, and Carol start to leave the Captain adds, "...And Stevens, try to stay out of trouble. I don't want to lose my pension because of you and your theories."

"Right, Captain C'mon guys, let's go Oh Captain, may I make a suggestion?"

"What is it," the Captain says.

"Well, it would be good to keep one of the uniforms here and keep one in the den here twenty-four seven."

"Okay, go on, get out of here."

Stevens speaks, "Don't forget the killer may try again on Friday, so we need to keep a sharp eye."

# CHAPTER FIVE

Thursday - 4:00 pm.

Stevens was upset as he, Rizzo, and Carol, walked out to his car. Rizzo tells him he is going to check something out, and he would see them in the morning. Stevens thought about how much time he had on the force and wondered if he was going to make it to his retirement date. Stevens was tired of the bureaucratic bullshit that the department tries to dish out by the toilet bowl full every day. He and Carol climb in the car and head toward Carol's apartment.

Carol seeing how upset Stevens was said, "Stevens, you're a good detective, have you ever thought about retiring from the force and opening an agency yourself?"

"Sure, all the time. I know just where I would open one too. Hawaii!"

"Hawaii? Why in the hell would you choose Hawaii? You know nothing about Hawaii."

"I'm fed up with digging my car out of snow in the wintertime. Dying of the humidity in the summertime."

"Listen, Stevens; you're upset when we get to my place why don't you come up for a drink."

"Sure, why not? That sounds great. I have to think about this case anyway."

They pulled up in front of the apartment. Carol noticed there were not any parking spots open. Carol said, "Why don't you let me off here, and I'll make us a couple of drinks while you park the car, okay?" He sees that Carol is still waiting for him to come around and open the door. He is pleased that Carol expects a little of the traditional ritual.

Stevens got out and went around and opened the door for Carol. She climbed out, and as she did, she found herself standing close to Stevens, and their eyes met. They both stood still for a moment, then Stevens spoke first.

"Well, I...a... better get the car parked. Are you sure you're going to be okay?"

"I'll have the drinks ready when you get upstairs."

As she turns and walks away, Stevens watches the poetry with which she moves as she walks to the front door. Stevens shakes his head, climbs back in the car, and goes and parks it. After five minutes, he finds a parking place not too far away. Stevens goes to the elevator and pushes the button for the third floor. It starts to rise to her third floor; he cannot help but think about Carol and where all this is going. The last time he felt this way was with Gloria. This time things would be different. At least that is what he wanted to think. The doors to the elevator swung open, and Stevens walked down the hall to the entrance of Carol's apartment and rang the bell. The door opened, Carol was standing with a drink in hand, a smile on her face.

"Well, I thought maybe you changed your mind and went home."

"Nope, here I am."

"Don't just stand there, come on in."

Stevens takes the drink from Carol and steps inside as Carol shuts the door. Stevens heads toward the living room and sits on the couch. Carol follows and sits next to him.

They both take a sip from their drinks. Both seem a little uncomfortable. Carol, because it has been a long time since she has had a man in her apartment, and Stevens because he is not sure this is right. After all, they are business associates sort of, and he knows they should keep it that way, but he enjoys her company and being around her. "Well, here we are..."

"Yeah, here we are...So tell me, do you think you'll catch the killer?" Carol speaks a little nervously.

"Oh yeah, there's no doubt about that, the real question is, will we catch him before he kills again."

"Were you serious about quitting?"

"Sure, why not. I think I'll finish this case and cash it all in." "What will you do?"

"Well, as I said before, maybe I'll open my agency in Hawaii."

"No! You couldn't do that, once a New Yorker, always a New Yorker." Carol is getting upset but tries to hold her temper.

Stevens replies, "Don't be too sure of what you're saying. I have had it with this city. I'm tired of the day to day bullshit."

"Yeah, but you couldn't leave this city, you love it too much."

"I don't know you can leave anyplace if you get fed up enough."

Carol looks at him strangely and says, "Well, I hope you stick around for a while."

There was a brief silence as they both stared at each other. Stevens spoke first. "Say I got a great idea."

"What's that?"

"Well, you heard the Captain, 'Take a couple of days off,' he said."

"Yeah, so, what's your idea?"

"Well, why don't you and I take a couple of days off and go upstate?"

"You mean just the two of us alone?"

"Yes, you know, as in you and me. I need to get away from the city for a couple of days, and I would love your company. I have a little cabin up North that I bought a few years ago. It is where I go to get away from it all, my sort of corner of the world. What do you say? I promise at the first sign of trouble. I'll call a policeman."

Carol looked at him knowing full well she was going to say yes, but not entirely sure she should. She smiles at what he just said and utters, "Well, now how could a lady refuse such a gallant offer. When do we leave?"

Stevens smiles and says, "In the morning, I'll pick you up a 7:00 am. Do you like the mountains?"

"I love them. I just have not had the time to go since I started college. I don't even know if I can take time off to go Stevens."

"Oh, sure, you can just tell them you have a sick relative to see."

"I'm afraid it's not as easy as that."

"Sure, it is, c'mon, what do you say ...take a chance...you won't be sorry."

Carol looked at Stevens, and he could tell by the look on her face that she knew she should go with him. At least that is what he was hoping. The Chief has been on his ass ever since the start of this case, and Stevens had enough.

Then Carol spoke, "Okay, let us go. I'll be ready at seven o'clock in the morning."

"Great, I'll pack a few things and be back to pick you up at about seven in the morning."

Stevens gets up to leave as he goes to the door; he suddenly realizes what he has just done. He stops at the door and turns back to Carol, who is by now standing at the kitchen door. "Wait a minute, what the hell am I talking about? I can't go."

"And tell me why not?" Carol says. "The Case, that's why not."

"What about it? Rizzo can handle it until we get back on Monday, can't he?"

"There may be something big coming down this weekend, and I want to be around for the finish."

"Wait a minute...Is this the same person who just a few minutes ago said, and I quote, 'I'm going to cash it in.'"

"Yeah, yeah, I know what I said, but I meant after the case had been solved. In the meantime, let us see what we can find out."

Carol smiles a knowing smile, walks up to Stevens, and says, "Don't worry, Stevens, I'll give you a rain check on the trip."

She puts her arms around his neck; gives him a friendly kiss. Stevens is not surprised over his next move; he puts his arms around her and kisses her back. It goes from an affectionate kiss to an involved one. When they finally stopped, they were staring at each other but not saying a word. They kissed again, this time they moved about as close as two people could get. When they stopped, Carol spoke first. "I'm sorry I shouldn't have done that."

"Yes, you should. You wanted to, and I wanted you to." "Your right, so now what happens?"

"What do you want to happen?" Without a word, Carol leaned her whole body next to Stevens and put her arms around him and kissed him. Stevens picked her up in his arms and carried her to the bedroom. He laid her down on the bed, looking at Carol for a time then lay down next to her.

It had been a long time since Carol got involved with a man. The last being her third year at NYU, her English teacher, he was always looking at her whenever she entered the room. She was twenty-one, and he was forty-one. He was married, that was one of the things that intrigued her about him. He started flirting the very first day, which should have been a warning for Carol. When your twenty-one, your feeling free and adventuresome. Besides, she liked the idea that an older man was attracted to her. She found him to be sexy, the way he always taught with a pipe in his mouth. She never saw him light it, but he still had it either in his hand or mouth. He always wore a tweed sports jacket with leather patches on the sleeve. Well, the relationship lasted six months before the wife found them out. At this point, she promptly divorces him. The school terminated his residency; they put Carol on a six-month probation. But that is a whole other story. It was quite an ordeal for Carol. It took her quite a while to get her mind back into her studies, and when she did, she decided there would be no men in her life until she finished school. Well, she almost made it.

They both lay on the bed, exploring each other's bodies; they began to feel drawn closer and closer to one another. Their problems began to dwindle into the deepest part of their psyche. In its place was the desire of a man and a woman for the baser things that keep us sane in a world full of insanity. Their lips met time and time again as their hands told them what was alive. Their animalistic pleasures seized them, and they drifted off into the world of fantasy and dreams.

# CHAPTER SIX

Friday - morning 8:00 am

As morning broke and the sun shone through Carol's bedroom, Stevens awoke and found Carol still sleeping beside him. He smiled as he realized all that happened the night before was real. Stevens brushed his hand over her forehead, moving the hair away from her beautiful eyes. As he leaned over to kiss her, her eyes opened, and the first thing she saw was the smile and looked of contentment in his eyes. She smiled as his lips kissed her, and she put her hands on each side of his cheeks and kissed him back. "Good morning, Stevens. Did you sleep well?"

Sam smiled and said, "I don't remember when I've slept as well, and you?"

"Hmmm, yes, me too. What time is it?"

Stevens looked at his watch and realized it was later then he wanted it to be. "Oh shit, we have to get going, this is Friday. It's also Halloween day, and we have a lot to do." Carol did not want to move, but she knew that Stevens was right and started to get up. "Do you want some breakfast?"

"No that's all right, mind if I use your phone, I want to call Rizzo. Wait, can I have a cup of coffee, black?"

"Sure thing." Carol put on her robe and went to the kitchen to make some coffee as Stevens dialed Rizzo at home. It rang twice before Rizzo picked it up.

"Hello, Rizzo? Well?"

Rizzo's voice is heard at the other end. "Hello, you old son of a bitch, should I guess where you spent the night? I knew you loved being around me, but you didn't have to go through all this to be part of the family."

"Ha, you know you are a funny man. It's not like that."

"Oh, you mean I'm going to have to defend the honor of the family name?"

"Rizzo, will you stop and listen to me for a minute?"

"Okay, okay. What's up?"

Stevens, by this time, was getting uptight about the whole situation he had put himself in, and he did not have time to think about it, so he just went on with the moment at hand. "How did you know where I was?"

"C'mon Stevens it didn't take a seasoned detective to figure it out when you didn't answer your phone this morning."

"Look, Rizzo; this is Friday. You DO remember that this is Friday, don't you?"

"Yes, Yes. I am not whacked out. Listen, I found out something yesterday, while you were on that holiday that you might find interesting."

"Tell me at the Spenser house. I'll meet you there in forty-five minutes."

"Yea...but Stevens, I wanted to tell you."

"Forty-five minutes at the Spenser house, tell me then, bye."

Stevens hung up the phone, got out of bed, and went to the dresser, and combed his hair. He saw a picture of Carol. She was standing there with an older man. He just smiled and continued combing his hair. Only then, Carol came into the room with some coffee and a fresh doughnut. Stevens looked at the doughnut and then back at Carol and said, "Where did you get the doughnuts this fast?"

"Well, I get them delivered every morning. There is this bakery downstairs;

the baker has the hot's for me. So, he does this little favor for me every morning before he opens." Stevens looked at Carol with a teasing smile on his face and said, "Oh, and what little favor do you do for him? Hmmm!"

"Very funny, you don't have to worry. The Baker is not my type."

"I'm glad."

Carol gives him one of those 'Oh you don't have to worry' looks and says, "So tell me what we are going to do first?"

"Well, to begin with, I'm going to jump in the shower, and we're going to meet Rizzo over at the Spenser house. Then we are going to take a little stroll down the passageways of that tunnel and see what we can find. If we are lucky, we'll find Mrs. Spencer alive."

Carol smiles, "Great sounds like we're going to have an interesting day ahead of us. What do you expect to find down there?"

"Well, I don't know for sure, but I'm hoping for a clue or two that will give us some more insight into this case. We have to find that killer today before it strikes again."

Carol goes to the closet and starts to dress, while Stevens goes into the shower. Just before they leave to go to the house, Stevens looks at Carol and says, "Listen, Carol, I want you to be careful today down in that tunnel. I don't want anything happening to you."

Carol turns and looks at Stevens, smiles, and says, "Oh Stevens, you're such a worrywart, you know that?"

"Yes, I know, but listen to me anyway... okay?"

"Okay, now c'mon, let's go."

Stevens walks over to Carol and kisses her on the cheek and says, "I'm ready; let's do it."

He puts his arm around Carol, and they both walked out the door and headed for the elevator. Rizzo is waiting on the steps of the Spenser house when Carol and Stevens arrive.

"Ah, I see you're on time for a change," Stevens says to Rizzo as he approaches the steps with Carol at his side.

"Yes, and you two look like a couple of newlyweds, oh well, let us get on with. To begin with, I have a news flash for you. Bob Mead and Ms. Spenser are NOT brother and sister...they are husband and wife, or at least they were before she disappeared."

"What the hell are you talking about, Rizzo?"

"Just like I said, they are not brother and sister. They are husband and wife; they have been married for three years. Their real names are William and Beth Mathis. He is in real estate, and she was working for him when they met three years ago."

"What else did you find out, and where do they fit into this case?"

"I'm coming to that; it seems that Tom Mead went to Mr. Mathis a year ago to find out who owns the property next store to him…it was for sale."

"Why would Tom Mead be interested in buying the property next to his?"

"I'm still working on that one."

Stevens looks at Carol, bewildered, and then back to Rizzo. "Well, do we have an address on Mr. and Mrs. Mathis?"

"Yes, 555 Park Ave Suite 404."

"Let's get a black and white over there right away and pick up Mr. Mathis."

"They're on their way."

"Good. Maybe we should also get a business address just in case Mr. Mathis is at his office."

"Get the number and have it called. Here's another interesting thing Mr. Mathis's secretary said he wouldn't be available for the next few days."

"Is that so well we'll see about that. In the meantime, let us go inside and see what we can find."

# CHAPTER SEVEN

Friday – Later that afternoon

It had been a long time since the old subway tunnels had any visitors, at least fifty years. That is except for this strange man-like creature that was roaming around there. As the tall, muscular figure of a man-like animal made his way to what had become his lair, we see a long tunnel way leading more profound and more in-depth down into the bowels of the earth. There is water dripping from the walls and ceilings of the passageway. As the creature moves down the conduit, his bull shaped head remains perfectly still. We see a wide opening just ahead of him on his right;

he passes through it and turns right. The passageway opens into a gigantic cavern. The cavern is shaped like a giant dome. The ceiling is partially covered with cement as if someone started to build, and when it was halfway done, they decided they did not want to finish it. The years weighed heavily on the old cement, and it had already started cracking in places. As the creature made his way to the center of the dome, he stopped long enough to pick up stray pieces of wood and carry them to the other side. He stacked them in the corner, along with other chunks he found since he had been there. There was a platform in the middle of the dome upon which stood a throne-like chair. That was his seating place. He sat down on the chair and looked around the dome like a king surveying his land. As he looked around, his eyes settled on the farthest part of the dome. Alongside one of the sides of the dome was Mrs. Mathis.

Chained to the wall, a prisoner in a World uninhabited by any other human.

Her face and clothes had mud and dirt all over them.

She looked like she had been dragged through the slimmest part of the old subway system. The creature stared at her for a moment, not saying anything. Then let out with a shriek that could be heard throughout the passageways. Mrs. Mathis watched in sheer terror as the creature got up and went to her side. As he approached her, her breathing became more and more erratic, until finally, she fainted. The creature moved closer, and with his hand, grabbed her hair and raised her head and looked at her, and then let her head drop back down and walked away, making her hang by the chains that were bound to her wrists.

In the meantime, again at the house, Rizzo was filling Carol and Stevens in on what he had discovered. "Another strange thing Stevens, I checked all the police reports of the murder victim, and there is one common denominator."

"What's that, Rizzo?"

"Well, all of the victims were into the occult. I mean, they played around with spells and stuff except for the Creature, of course."

Stevens and Carol looked at each other for a moment, and then Carol asked, "Why don't we find out if Mr. and Mrs. Mathis are into the occult?"

Stevens turned and looked at Carol and then spoke to Rizzo, "Good idea, Carol, and while you're at it, Rizzo, find out if there had been any strange murders before Mr. Spenser bought his house, anywhere in the city. I want to know what we are up against here. The chief is going to be on my ass unless I can turn up some hard evidence, so let us get cracking on this."

"Right Stevens, I'll get on it right away."

Rizzo turns and heads out the door. Stevens turns to Carol and realizes she moved to the table to stare at the map of the tunnel.

"What's up, Carol?"

"Nothing Stevens.   except I was just wondering."

"Wondering what, Carol?"

"Well, if there is A Minotaur, and he did take Mrs. Spenser...er...Mathis down into the tunnels. According to legend, he would take her to his lair. I was checking the map for someplace that could act as a lair."

"And what did you find out?"

"Well, nothing shows on the map that suggests there could be a place that could be used for that, but that doesn't mean that there isn't one."

"I guess that means we'll have our work cut out for us. Where do you think we should start?"

Just then, patrolman York walked into the library. "Excuse me, Lt.!"

Stevens turned toward the door and said, "Yes, what do you want York?"

"Well, Lt. There is a phone call for you in the hall. It is the desk, Sgt. at the station house. He says it's important."

"Okay, tell him I'll be right there. Carol, you hold that thought while I am gone. Keep looking for anything that could be used as a Lair."

Carol goes over to the table to check out the map while Stevens was on the phone. Stevens tells Officer York to wait there while he went outside to the other room where the phone was. He did not want to leave Carol unprotected.

"Hello, yes this is Lt. Stevens, what do you want? What! Okay, I will take the call, it's right around the corner from here. Thanks, have the boys from the lab meet me there, right. Bye."

Stevens hung up the phone and headed back into the den, where Carol was looking over the map. "Okay, Carol, you stay here I'll be back in about an hour. Our killer has struck again. This time it is on Remsen Street, just around the corner. The boys from the lab are going to meet me there."

"I'm coming with you, Stevens."

"No, Carol, I need you here checking that map out, besides this is official police business." Going out the door, Stevens sees patrolman York.

"York, station yourself in the den with Carol, and don't let her out of your sight."

"Right, Lt."

# CHAPTER EIGHT

Friday – Early afternoon.

Stevens turned on to Remsen Street he could see three patrol cars and a lot of people hanging around the front entrance to a brownstone house. The media had already gotten there. They were taking pictures of what looks like the remains of a body. They had the area roped off, but the people were pushing and shoving. Stevens made his way through the crowd and came upon a uniformed policeman. He was a tall man, much taller than Stevens. The policeman had his back to the group with his hands extended, trying to hold the masses back. Stevens tapped the officer on the shoulder, and when he turned around, Stevens stuck his badge in his face and told him to let him in.

"Go under my arms, Lt. Sir."

As Stevens made his way over toward the body, he could hear the ambulance in the distance. As he approached the body, he could see that the M O was the same as the others. It was a male Caucasian.

Who looked to be about 37 or 38 years old and about 6 feet? His head had been twisted around, he was lying on his stomach, and his head was facing up. Stevens looked around for the officer that found the body. A young-looking patrolman was sitting on the curb by himself, wiping his face with his handkerchief. Stevens walked up to him. "Excuse me, are you the patrolman that found the body?" The young policeman turned and looked up and recognized who was talking to him and jumped up and said, "I'm sorry, sir, yes, I found the body.

My name is patrolman Frank Meyers with an S, sir."

"Relax, son, and tell me exactly what you found when you got here."

"Well, sir, like I told Officer Kelly, my supervisor. The body was lying over there, among the trash cans. At first, I thought it was just some wino passed out for the night. When I got closer, I could see that his head was twisted around, and he was lying on his stomach. I went to the call box over there and called it in."

"While you waited for the back-up team to arrive, did you touch anything or move the body at all?"

"No, sir, I didn't. We were taught at the academy not to touch anything or move anything at the crime scene, only secure it."

Stevens smiled and said, "Good, when you first arrived on the scene, did you see anyone leaving?"

"I did see someone go up that alley and disappear."

He pointed to the alley across the street. Stevens walked across the street and looked up the alleyway for a minute and then returned to the patrolman.

"Can you tell me what he or she looked like?"

"Well, sir, it was a man, that's all I can tell you for sure, but er..." He hesitated as if he was not sure about what he saw. Stevens picked up on it and continued.

"Well, what is it son, what did he look like?"

"I only saw him for a minute, and it was from behind. He looked to be about seven feet tall."

"What was he wearing?"

"Well, that's what I'm not sure about. I mean, he looked like he was wearing a long overcoat, and the more I looked at him, the more it looked like a robe or gown of some sort."

"Robe, are you sure?"

"Yes, sir, and his head looked big for the body it was on. I mean, it looked out of proportion with the body."

Stevens not believing what he just heard took down all the information. "Thank you, kid, is there anything else you saw or discovered when you got here?"

"No, sir, that's all."

Stevens told the patrolman to go back to his beat, and he would check with him later. It was around eight p.m. by the time Stevens got back to the Spenser house. The patrolman at the front door looked as though he was about to fall on his face. It must have been a long day for him too. Stevens knew how he was feeling. As he approached the top of the steps to the front door, the patrolman recognized Stevens and opened the door to let him pass.

"Evening York, how's it going?" Stevens said.

"Fine, sir, the lady is still inside, and Lt. Rizzo is with her." "Thank you, York. When do you get relieved?"

"Any time now, sir."

"Good go home and get some sleep; you look done in," Stevens said as he made his way down the corridor to the den.

As he entered the den, he started smiling. Both Rizzo and Carol had fallen asleep, Carol on the couch, Rizzo on the Chair. Stevens went to the couch and put his hand on Carol's shoulder at the same time she turned and smiled up at him and said, "Is it morning yet?"

Stevens replied, "You're a light sleeper remind me never to try to rob your apartment, at least while you're in it anyway."

Carol smiled, "Wouldn't get much anyway. So, what's up?" "Well, our friend struck again, this time a little closer to home."

"Oh no, that's awful how far from here?"

"Two blocks over toward the bridge."

"Are you sure it's him?"

"Yep same m.o. No doubt about it."

Rizzo hearing Stevens talking stirs and says, "Well, what's next?"

There is a silence, as both Rizzo and Carol looked at Stevens, waiting to hear what he had to say. Stevens is pacing back and forth across the den, scratching the back of his head with his hand. Finally, snapping his fingers and stopping in front of the library wall. He is looking at the wall with a smile. Then he turned and faced the both of them and said, "There is only one thing we can do, and that is to go into the tunnel and find the murderer whoever or whatever it is."

Rizzo jumped up and smiled and looked at Carol then back at Stevens and said, "Great, when do we start?"

Carol just sat on the couch, looked at Stevens with that determined look on her face, and said, "Okay, when do we leave?"

Stevens looked at both of them then at the maps on the table, then back at Carol. "Well, Carol, do you have all the passageways memorized?"

"I think so...yes...I do."

Then Stevens spoke, "Since he already struck earlier today, I don't think he'll strike any more tonight. So, we will all get some sleep and meet back at the house in the morning at nine a.m. and start fresh. It's going to be a long day tomorrow."

Rizzo looked at Stevens said, "Well, you know he struck a day early. He is out of his pattern; do you think he'll strike again tomorrow?"

Stevens speaks, "No, I don't, and I think he is finished for the time being anyway. Let us go home and get some sleep."

They both agree with Stevens, and Rizzo is the first to leave. "Catch you guys in the morning. Then with a smile, he says, and do not be late, you two."

Stevens gives him the old oh get out of here jester with his hand, and Rizzo leaves. Stevens turned to Carol and said, "C'mon, let me go ahead and drop you off it's going to be a long day tomorrow." They both head for the door. Stevens said goodbye to the officers who had to stay all night and told them to keep their eyes open for anything strange.

# CHAPTER NINE

Saturday – Morning -9 am.

Stevens, Carol, and Rizzo met promptly at nine in the morning. They were all bright-eyed and bushy-tailed and ready to start the adventure. They went up the stairs and into the building. They passed two new Uniformed Policemen watching the front. Stevens spoke first, "Everything okay, guys?"

The first Policemen answered quickly, "Yes, sir, everything is and has been quiet all night long."

"Okay, let us move out, Rizzo, you follow behind Carol. Carol, you stay in the middle, it will be safer that way. I will take the lead. You tell me which direction to go."

"Okay, let us go, Stevens. This is not the Army. You're beginning to sound like a general."

"I'm sorry guys, got a little carried away. I want to make sure you understand the danger involved in this journey. Let us go."

Stevens, Carol, and Rizzo walked toward the wall that led to the tunnel. Rizzo pulled the book that separated the wall from the rest of the house. The wall pulled apart, leaving a doorway that was going to lead the three of them on an unknown journey Stevens stepped through with his gun drawn followed by Carol and Rizzo.

In the meantime, in another one of the tunnels, we see Bob Mead (aka Bill Mathis) making his way to the Lair of the Minotaur. As he enters the Lair, he considers the Minotaur sitting on his throne looking like the Lord of his kingdom, which of course, is what he was in this case. As Bill Mathis approached the throne, he greets the Minotaur with a bow and says, "Well, have you brought her here?" The Minotaur, without saying a word, looks and points to the far corner of the Lair, where Ms. Spenser (aka Mrs. Beth Mathis) is chained to the wall. One of the strange things about the Minotaur is that it seems to understand everything that Bill Mathis says to him but never speaks. He seems to have an extremely high intellect, almost as if he is communicating as though he has mental telepathy. The Minotaur sat very still on his throne as Bill Mathis walked over to the wall where Mary Mathis was chained.

As he approached her, she looked up and looked straight into Bill's eyes, saying, "Why are you doing this to me? You know I love only you."

Mr. Mathis speaks, "Don't lie to me; I found you in bed with him the night before I had him taken care of."

"That's not true; I was only..."

"Shut-up, you... you...bitch."

Mary started to cry and let her head drop down on to her chest while crying even louder. Bill moved closer and grabbed her hair and lifted her head so he could get a good look at her.

"Now, you cry, you want mercy. All you women cry when your caught and do not know what else to do. Well, it will not work this time. I am going to take care of you later in my own time and in my way. Ha." As if he heard something, he turns and looks at the Minotaur. They stare at one another for a minute, and then Bill sounding a little crazed, says, "So, we have visitors to our little world hmmm." Looking at the Minotaur, Bill says, "C'mon take her with us. We don't want to be found just yet."

The Minotaur goes to the wall and rips the chains out, freeing Mary. He grabs her by the arms and pulls her with them as they leave the dome area to another part of the tunnel and disappear down the Passage.

Stevens and Carol and Rizzo advance down the passageways across tracks into another tunnel. A couple of hours of exploring had passed without discovering anything stopped. Stevens speaks first, "Well, we're not doing any good, are we?"

"We knew this wasn't going to be easy, Stevens." Rizzo replies and then continues, "Why don't we call it a day and try again tomorrow?"

"Wait, here's an opening up ahead let's check it out first, then we'll head back."

As they go through the opening, they see a considerable dome area. Carol speaks, "Say, Stevens, this is the kind of place the Minotaur would inhabit if he were going to live some place down here. Let us check it out."

Stevens is looking around the room. Finally, he stops and says, "Okay. You know, Carol, you may be right about him. Check out this throne-like chair on this platform."

Carol moves closer and inspects it. "Yeah, this does look like the place he would come."

"Hey, Stevens, check these footprints in the mud over here by the wall."

"It looks like someone had been here recently. It looks like three somebodies. There are three sets of footprints, and one of them looks like a woman's."

"Yea and they lead off in this direction," Rizzo says, pointing to the doorway on the other side of the room. Stevens speaks, "Say why don't we mark this spot off where we can continue tomorrow and call it a day. I have a feeling we are going to need more people than we have now. Maybe we could get a couple of police officers stationed here in case the Creature comes back. Let us head back." Rizzo speaks first, "Sounds like a good idea; my feet are killing me."

"Oh, Rizzo, you are such a wuss, I swear. I want to go on; this is getting exciting." Carol says.

"No, I think it's best if we start fresh tomorrow morning. I'll talk to the chief and see if we can get more people to come with us." Stevens leads them back the way they came, heading back to the den. They passed a doorway that they did not see before when they were coming down to this place. "Say, here is a passageway I think we should check out first," Stevens says.

They head through the door and down the passageway about a hundred feet or so. They come to a dead-end; there is a wall in front of them. There is also a ladder stuck to the wall leading up.

Stevens looks above and sees a sewer cover. He grabs the ladder. "Hold up guys I'll check it out." Stevens climbs up the ladder. After a couple of minutes, he can lift the cover and lay it aside while he climbs up onto the street. After looking around, he shouts down the opening, "Come on up, it's okay."

Carol and Rizzo climb up the ladder and put the lid back in place and look round. Rizzo speaks, "Where are we?" Stevens says, "Well if I'm right, this is the alley where that thing disappeared after yesterday's murder. It was the alley that leads to the street where the murder victim was found, the same alley that the Policeman reported to Me yesterday that he saw someone go into and disappear."

"Well, at least we are back onto the street again. Now, if I could find my car, I could go home and take a shower and get some sleep." Rizzo complains.

"Yeah, well, we could meet back here in the morning, say around ten a.m. What do you say? Is that late enough for everyone to get some sleep?"

Carol and Rizzo reply in unison, "Sounds good to me." They look at each other and laugh.

Stevens says, "Boy, you two guys are related."

Steven and Rizzo both smiled. Three of them headed off to the street where the cars were parked. Tomorrow was going to be an exciting day. Stevens had to make a call to the chief and see if he could spare more men. Stevens wanted to get a couple of men in the domed area to watch for the Creature.

He knew the chief was not going to like this, but what could he do. While Stevens drove Carol home, they chatted.

Stevens spoke first, "Carol, you know I don't know what's in store for all of us tomorrow. You still have time to back out of this. I'll understand."

"You must be kidding; this is the most excitement I've been exposed to in a long time." With that, Carol cuddled up next to Stevens in the front seat with her head lying on his shoulder as he drove her home. It did not take long for her to fall asleep.

# CHAPTER TEN

Saturday – Morning 10 am

Today was going to prove to be an exciting day. At least that is what Stevens thought as the three of them stood over the utility hole cover, they discovered yesterday.

"Okay, now does everyone know what they are supposed to do?"

Carol was the first to speak, "Yes, I'm going to stay behind you where you think I'll be safe."

"Right and guess who is in charge of the map, you," Rizzo says with a knowing smile.

"All right, let's go."

Rizzo speaks, "Say, Stevens, I meant to ask you, did you get a hold of the chief, and did he say he would put some men down there to help us?"

Stevens replied, "Yep, the chief yelled and scream, but after everything was said and done, he said he would put some men down there."

Carol and Rizzo followed Stevens down the utility hole to the sewer and into the passageway. They headed down the tunnel to the Dome area, where they left off yesterday.

Before you could say Ishkabible, they were standing in a dome-like area where they assumed the creature lived. Two patrolmen were standing over by the platform. Stevens spoke first, "Okay, men look alive. Have you seen or heard anything?"

While in another part of the tunnel, the creature, Mr. Mathis, and their latest soon to be victim meet to decide Mrs. Mathis's fate. "Well, my dear, have you had enough time to think about what you have done to me and your future?"

"Bob, I'm trying to tell you it was all a mistake and I'm sorry. I did not mean to hurt you. I promise it will never happen again."

"Oh, I know it won't. I am going to make sure of that. Turning to the creature, Bob says, mister creature, do you mind doing what you do best?"

The Creature looked at Mr. Mathis and then at Mrs. Mathis. Slowly he moved over to where Mrs. Mathis was tied up. With one swift movement of his body, he picks up Mrs. Mathis twists her head off her shoulders. Mr. Mathis watches the body fall to the ground while the creature was still holding the head he turns and shows it to him. Mr. Mathis has a crazed smile on his face as he says, "Dispose of the body like the rest of the ones you took care of before."

With the head in one hand, the Creature picks up the body with the other hand and disappears down the passageway. Mr. Mathis starts laughing in a crazed sort of way that echoes throughout the rest of the tunnel.

Just then, at another part of the tunnel, Stevens, Rizzo, and Carol are talking. "Did you hear that?" Stevens says.

"No. What was it some noise?" Answers Rizzo. "I'm not sure it sounded as if someone was laughing. Anyway, let us go this way." Pointing to the passageway to the left, Stevens is listening for any more noises. He does not hear any. Stevens turned toward the others and continued, "You guy stay here and keep your eyes open." Carol speaks, "Say, Stevens, according to the map

I've been looking at; we should be going this way." Pointing in the opposite direction in which Stevens was going.

Stevens turns and heads in the direction of Carol, "Well, let's stick to the map." With that, he starts down the passageway with Carol and Rizzo. Stevens leads the way. As he passes through the doorway, he comes face to face with the Creature. He does not believe what he is seeing. The Creature, with one swift movement of his hand, pushes Stevens backward into Carol and Rizzo. All three fall as the Creature disappears down the other passageway. Stevens is the first to get up. He helps Carol up and says, "Did you see him? Did you?"

Carol speaks first, "All I saw was you flying into me and knocking me down."

"Stay here; I'm going after him." Stevens took off in the direction of the Creature. Stevens did not know what he was going to do when he caught up with him (like a dog chasing a car wheel) but still had to try. The Creature knew every foot of the different passageways. He had been down there for a long time and knew where to go to be safe. If he did not want to be found, he would not be. Stevens made so many turns in so many passageways that he lost his way.

When he finally stopped and took stock of things, he knew he was lost. Stevens started trying to remember the map in the library and the way it looked arranged on the table.

Then he walked back in the direction of the library, at least in the direction he thought the library was. Thinking about the creature and the way it stared at him before it pushed him down and ran off. It did not look anything like the pictures he saw in books when he read the stories about him in school. After a few turns and going through different passageways, he heard a female's voice calling out. "Stevens, where are you? Stevens answer me, dammit." Stevens smiles and shouts back, "I'm down here, keep going straight, and you will find me." A few minutes later, the three were back together again.

"Say Stevens what the hell happened back there."

Rizzo speaks, "All I saw was Carol falling into me, and I fell, next thing I knew, you were gone."

"You didn't see the Creature either?"

"Nope, I didn't see anything except Carol's back flying into me and me hitting the floor."

"Well, the Creature is no longer a theory. I saw it." Rizzo speaks, "Great! Is that what we're going to tell the chief?"

"Yes! Just not right now. I want some more information about Mr. & Mrs. Mathis. Let us head back to the Library."

"Ok."

They all turned around and followed Rizzo back to the Library. When they entered through the Library wall, Stevens was the first one to speak, "Say, Carol, can you check and see what they have in the kitchen in the way of drinks and food? We may be here for a while."

"Sure, Stevens, not a problem." She turns and heads to the kitchen.

"Say, Rizzo, what did you find out about the Mathis's?" Rizzo takes out his notebook from his back pocket and flips through some pages. "Well, I have here is that Mr. & Mrs. Mathis had been married about ten years when Mrs. met Bob Mead. Shortly after that, they had an affair, according to Bob Meads neighbor Mrs. Sullivan, a widower."

Stevens says, "Mr. Mathis must have found out about it and decided to do something. He couldn't just kill Bob Mead without throwing suspicion on himself so, enter the creature."

Rizzo speaks again, "Yea, but Stevens, how did he get the creature here in the first place?"

"That part is easy." Says Carol as she reenters from the kitchen with a tray. "Say, Stevens, all I could find was a couple of sprites and a coke. I did find some bread, so I made three peanut butter and jelly sandwiches. Sorry, guys, that's all there was."

"That's fine." Says Stevens and then continuing, he says, "What's that part you were saying about it being easy?"

"Well don't forget we found the book with incantations in the house, so one of two things are certain, one Bob Mead brought the creature here from the past with the book or two he was here before Bob Mead bought the place and already hiding in the subway system."

"Which means the creature could have been brought here by the previous owner, and Bob Mead met him when he moved in," says Rizzo.

"Something is wrong with that theory," Carol Says. Stevens and Rizzo, at the same time, say, "What's that?"

Carol continues, "I'm not sure, but I'd like to know how the Minotaur was controlled and who controlled him."

"Well, sounds to me like nobody controls him," Rizzo says. Stevens chimes in, "What makes you say that?"

Rizzo continues, "Well, if he was here when the last owner owned this house according to the records, we have on him, he was found with his head twisted around like Bob Mead. That tells me the creature killed him—same M.O. We know how Bob Mead was killed, and it looks like the creature did him in too. Going by what I've told you, the creature isn't controlled at all but kills at will."

"Very good, Rizzo, that makes sense," Stevens says. Continuing Stevens says, "That would mean that who brought forth the creature to the present didn't know they couldn't control it, and that's why they died." Stevens continues, "If that's the case then all these murders where random killings, so Mr. Mathis found out about the Mrs. and Bob Mead having an affair and somehow made the opportunity happen for the creature to kill Bob Mead and kidnap Mrs. Mathis."

Carol smiles and says, "Well, if all that is true, all we have to do is find the creature and prove that Mr. Mathis had Bob Mead and Mrs. Mathis were all killed by the creature piece of cake."

"Yeah, right, piece of cake," Stevens repeats. They both smiled at each other.

"So how do we do that?" Rizzo says.

"I haven't figured that one out yet. I do know the first thing we have to do. Catch the creature to prevent him from killing again."

"I repeat, how do we do that?" Rizzo says.

"I don't have all the answers yet Rizzo I'm going to have to think about that one," Stevens says.

"Carol, do you have any idea on the subject?" Carol speaks. "Well, according to Greek mythology, he was beaten to death by Theseus, but the fact that he traveled into the present by some chant, I don't know how impervious he is or how we could kill him. I'll need some time to check it out."

"Okay, why don't you do that while Rizzo and I see what we can find out?"

Carol replies, "Ok, I'll go to the New York Public Library and check and see what I can find out. They would have the most extensive books on the subject." She turns and leaves.

"Ok, Rizzo, let's go over what we do know about this case." "And that is?" Rizzo says.

"Well, first of all, we know somehow, he was brought here through a chant, and second he doesn't kill every twenty-eight days as we thought, but whenever he feels like it. Third, he cannot be controlled by any one person. Lastly, Mr. Mathis is somehow involved with at least one of the killings."

"Well, knowing all that Stevens, maybe we should find out which incantation brought him here, and in that way, we may be able to find a way to reverse it."

"Good idea," Stevens says and continues, "I think Carol will be taking care of that end, we should be concentrating on Mr. Mathis and his involvement. Let us check upstairs; maybe we can find something that will help us solve this mystery."

"Say, Stevens, I know this is a little late to be asking, but you saw the creature, what did he look like?"

"All I can tell you is that he was big and did have the head of a bull as the story says. The rest of him looked like a man's body; only he wore a robe instead of clothes."

They both headed up the stairs, Stevens speaks first. "Okay, Rizzo, you take the first room on the left, and I'll check this one out." He points to the first room on the right. Stevens continues, "Look for anything that might tell us how they used those incantation books pictures anything."

"Okay, Stevens, I'm on it." Rizzo goes into the first room, and Stevens disappears into the other room.

Meanwhile, deep below the streets of New York, the creature has plans of his own.

The Creature and Mr. Mathis are having a meeting. The Creature speaks first, "You said if I helped you, you would help me to get back home. I will help you now; it's your turn."

"Things got complicated, so we have a couple more people to get rid of first. When that happens, I will get you home, I promise."

"You made this complicated; this is not the way it was supposed to happen. I want to go home now. If you do not send me home, I'll kill you and find a way myself."

"Ok don't go crazy on me, I'll go and get the book, and we will do it now."

Mathis leaves the tunnel and heads up toward the passageways looking for the entrance to the room upstairs. Unbeknownst to Mathis, he enters the room where Rizzo is searching. Rizzo thinking it is Stevens turns toward the door when it opens, and in a flash, Mathis sees him and turns and runs down the hall where he runs into Stevens coming out of the other room. Stevens grabs him and slams the cuffs on him.

"Whoa. Mathis, where do you think you are going?" Rizzo comes running up behind Mathis, saying, "Good Job Stevens, you got him. Now we can ask him some questions before we take him in for the murders."

Mathis says, "What Murders, I didn't do anything wrong it was that Creature, not me."

"Yeah, right," Rizzo continues, "And if the Creature could speak, he would say he didn't do it, you did."

Stevens speaks, "Tell me something, Mr. Mathis, how did that Creature get here, to begin with?"

Mathis says, "That I don't know I met him when I was trying to sell the house for Mr. Mead."

"So, who killed Mr. Mead?" asked Rizzo. "The creature."

Rizzo continues, "What about your wife, where is she?"

"I swear I don't know I do know the Creature took her, but I don't know where."

Rizzo speaks, "You're lying. You know where she is." Stevens says, "Mrs. Mathis is dead." Stevens waits to see the reaction on Mathis's face. After about a minute, Mathis spoke with a crazy smile on his face.

"I knew she was dead because I had the creature kill her. She was cheating on me with Tom Mead. So, I had the Creature, Kill Tom, too. I had the creature kill the other ones so that it would like a random killing by a crazy person."

"I think we heard enough Rizzo. Have him put all that in writing and sign it. Then call the chief and have him send over the Patrol car. We'll cart Mr. Mathis off to Jail."

"After all this excitement, I wonder how Carol is doing at the library."

"This isn't over yet. Rizzo, we still have to go back down to the tunnels one more time and find the creature. First, we have to find Carol and see if she finds anything we can use against the Creature.

"Someone call me?"

Stevens and Rizzo turned and saw Carol standing there. Stevens spoke first. "Oh, you're back, did you find out anything at the library that we could use to kill or catch this creature so that it won't kill anyone else?"

"Other than what I told you the first time we met. The legend says that Theseus beat the Minotaur to death in his sleep. I don't think he inherited any special powers when he was transported from the past to the present."

"If what you say is true, then if I have to, I could kill him with my gun. That's a good thing; I feel better already." Just then, Rizzo chimed in, "Remember Stevens, we still have to find him in the tunnel." Rizzo picks up a camera to see if he could get a picture for proof.

After the Police picked-up Mr. Mathis and took him downtown for booking Stevens, Rizzo and Carol headed back into the tunnel to locate the creature. After about an hour of weaving left right and down the tunnel passageways, they came upon what they guessed was the Lair for the Creature. As they entered the tunnel dome, they saw the Creature sitting on the rock in the center of the room. The Creature spoke much to their surprise.

"Come in. I have been expecting you."

They were all shocked to find out that he spoke none more so than Carol, who spoke first. "Where are you from?"

"I am from a different time and place. Can you return me to that place?"

"Place?" Stevens spoke, "We can but will not be able to."

"Why not?"

"You have committed a crime in our time and place and must pay the price."

Carol spoke next, "You must atone for your crime."

"What crime did I commit?"

"You have committed the crime of murder." This time it was Rizzo who spoke.

"But I have only done what was requested of me so that I may be sent back to where I came."

"In the eyes of the people that govern this world in which you reside at present, you have committed the crime of murder for which could carry a death sentence. We cannot allow you to return to your world."

"If I cannot return to my world, I must die in yours." He stands and starts walking toward Stevens. Stevens pulls his gun and warns the creature to stop, or he will shoot. The beast kept walking toward him with his hands raised.

Stevens fires his gun twice, hitting the being in the chest. The creature falls to the ground, at which point Rizzo runs toward the body and pulls out the camera and clicks a few pictures, saying, "I need these for my scrapbook."

As he snapped the photos, the creature on the ground started to fade away. Stevens and the rest stand there in total amazement and wonder. Now there is nobody on the ground. The body has completely disappeared.

Rizzo speaks, "Great now, how are we going to explain this to the Chief?"

Stevens says, "I don't know, but you better hope those pictures come out."

Carol speaks next, "I can, I think when you shot him, you also killed the spell that brought him here, and his body went back to where it came. I hope it stays there."

# EPILOGUE

Well, after an hour in the chief's office trying to explain this case, Stevens finally explained it in a way that the boss could accept it. He showed him the pictures Rizzo took. So, Stevens and Rizzo were off the hook. Now that the case was officially closed, Stevens could put in for his retirement.

Rizzo was shocked and asked Stevens what he was to do now. Stevens told him he had put enough money aside over the years to open his detective agency here in New York, and he could not wait to get started.

"Stevens, what happened about your idea of going to Hawaii, Carol asked."

"I'll tell you, Carol, sweetheart. It was something you said about missing New York after I left. I thought long and hard about that, and you were right. Only that is not all of it.

"I'm not ready to leave you behind, and since you wouldn't leave school to go with me and I wouldn't ask you to, I figured I would stick around here for a while."

Carol smiled and walked toward Stevens, Stevens met her halfway, and they embraced and kissed. I guess this adventure is just beginning.